JONNY BRIGGS AND THE GHOST

"It's a ghost," said Jonny Briggs, "with a football under its arm."

Everyone in Port Street has been talking about the ghost for days, and nearly everyone except Jonny seems to have seen it. But soon he's forced to go ghost hunting – with surprising results.

JONNY BRIGGS
and the
GHOST

Joan Eadington

Illustrated by William Marshall

as told in Jackanory by
Bernard Holley

BBC/KNIGHT BOOKS

Copyright © Joan Eadington 1978
Illustrations © British Broadcasting Corporation 1978

First published 1978 by the British Broadcasting Corporation

This edition published 1984 by the
British Broadcasting Corporation/Knight Books
Second impression 1985

British Library C.I.P.

Eadington, Joan
    Jonny Briggs and the ghost.
    I. Title
    823'.914[J]   PZ7

    ISBN 0-340-35338-4
          0-563-20341-2 BBC

Printed and bound in Great Britain for the British
Broadcasting Corporation, 35 Marylebone High Street,
London W1M 4AA and Hodder and Stoughton
Paperbacks, a division of Hodder and Stoughton Ltd.,
Mill Road, Dunton Green, Sevenoaks, Kent (Editorial
Office: 47 Bedford Square, London, WC1 3DP) by
Richard Clay (The Chaucer Press) Ltd,
Bungay, Suffolk

1

Jonny Briggs was extremely proud of his golden belt. His dad said it must be the very best belt in the whole of Yorkshire. But when he first started wearing it at school, there was trouble.

Some people were jealous and kept trying to get it off him, and once someone tried to crumple it up and stamp on it.

Then, one day, Miss Broom said to the class: "Seeing there seems to have been such a fuss about Jonny Briggs's belt, and seeing that he made it himself and it was his own idea in the first place – I've decided you can *all* make a golden belt if you want to. You can make it of anything you like: cloth, paper, cardboard, or even string. But it must be a *gold* belt, and Jonny Briggs can say which one he likes the best." (Then Miss Broom added under her breath: "and after that, perhaps we'll get some *peace*!")

Jonny was over the moon with delight. It was the first time in his life he had been allowed to choose anything at school. Lily Spencer was always choosing things. She chose the best painted Easter Egg. And even Pam had chosen the best cress grown on blotting paper. And – come to think of it – even those terrible twins Jinny and Josie had once been chosen to decide the nicest paper flower.

Jonny ran extra quickly back from school that day. Everything seemed to be perfect. Everyone had been fussing round him asking the best way to make a proper gold belt, and as if that wasn't enough, Pam's big brother Stew had sent a message for him to go and play footy in the park straight after tea because he – Jonny Briggs – was the best football player of the lot . . .

Life was paradise!

He almost skipped in at the back door. His gold belt sparkled in the last of the day's sunshine. He felt ready for any adventure in the world, and ran into the kitchen bubbling over with the good news.

But everyone was so busy talking they completely ignored him. They seemed to have forgotten him entirely. There was his sister Rita, and his brothers Albert and Humph, and they were all talking about the ghost.

Jonny groaned. He wasn't really surprised they were talking about the ghost. Everybody in Port Street seemed to be talking about it at the moment, and nearly everyone seemed to have seen it except him.

He stood there and watched them all, gabbling on as they sat round the kitchen table. Albert's floppy black hair was bobbing all over the place as he energetically described a most amazing creature with huge red eye sockets and a great moaning voice. . . .

"It's very, very thin, too," said Albert, stuffing his mouth with toast as if it was his last meal on earth. "It's the ghost of a boy who starved to death in this very house, a hundred and fifty years ago."

"These houses weren't built then," said Humph, giving him a calm monkey-faced look. "A hundred and fifty years ago it was all fields round here! And all that mysterious rattling we heard last night was Charlie-next-door, falling off the slates on the wash-house roof. He'd locked himself out and was trying to climb in."

Jonny grinned. He noticed that two of his sisters, Sandra and Pat, had already had their tea and hurried off out again. He was glad because it meant there was more space. And when there weren't so many of them eating at the same time it meant he didn't have to try and calculate how far the food was going to go and how much of it he was going to get.

Sandra and Pat never got mixed up in family arguments. Pat, who worked at the chemists', spent her time thinking about her boy friend, and ice skating at Billingham

Forum. And Sandra usually disappeared to see their married sister Marilyn – because Marilyn let her cook lots of curries.

So with those two out of the way, it just left Rita. . . .

Nothing'll ever shift her, thought Jonny sadly, as he sat down and crunched at a piece of toast with a charred black crust which Rita had just handed to him as if she was the Queen of Sheba. He stared at her extra hard and wished he had ray-gun eyes that could make enemies disappear. She was standing there now, with a slimming biscuit in one hand, while with her other hand she filled in her eyebrows with an eyebrow pencil. He noticed that her new eyebrows gave her a very surprised look.

"My friend Mavis says it's a ghost with its head tucked underneath its arm," said Rita.

"That's not its *head*," said Jonny, going quite red with indignation. "It's the ghost of a footballer! Ask anyone in this street and they'll tell you the same. It's a *football* under his arm. And it's no good grinning like that our Rita – it *is*!" He looked at them all disgustedly. They were *all* grinning.

"How do *you* know?" spluttered Albert, as

he laughed a shower of damp crumbs onto the kitchen floor. "You're the only person left who hasn't seen it, our Jonny."

It was about a week since the ghost stories had first started. Jonny began to wonder what he'd really do if he saw one. Would he be scared out of his wits like Harry Prince across the road, or would he be so interested in seeing it that he'd forget to be frightened at all? It wasn't often you came across ghost footballers; he was supposed to be one of those old ones like the 1950 Works Team on the photo in mam and dad's bedroom. Pamela Dean at school said the ghost wore black, knee-length trousers like an old-fashioned referee and that he had huge old-fashioned boots with toe caps. But strangest of all . . . he had no head! Just this thin body, all long and bony, carrying a football under its arm. . . . Except when it was full moon.

When it was full moon the ghost's head came back. He had a very pale face and long black beard . . . both the Brown brothers had seen him at full moon and swore to it.

But Lily Spencer – whose mother was a nurse – said it was the ghost of the first woman footballer who played in a team called Ironopolis hundreds of years ago and she *did* have a head because if a ghost hadn't got a head it wouldn't be able to walk about properly.

Jonny finished his tea. He felt as if he hadn't had any. When mam made the tea his gold belt felt as if it would snap because his tummy was full to bursting. But when Rita was in charge, his gold belt slipped about because it had nothing to lean against and he could push both his hands underneath it. He gulped three large mouthfuls of orange squash to fill himself up, then dashed out to the park to play footy.

Halfway down Port Street, he bumped right into his mother! She was coming home from her job. She worked part-time at an ironmongers', selling nails and spades and kitchen taps and lawn mowers. Jonny wished he worked in a place like that instead of being at school.

"Where do you think you're going in such a hurry?" said his mam suspiciously. She was always a bit narky when she came back from work. She always said it was because she felt extra tired. Then she said:

"Did Rita get any tea ready?"

"Not much," said Jonny. "She made toast ..." And he began to rub his neck gently – just under his chin. It was the part where his throat was still sore from golloping down Rita's toasted charcoal.

"Trust her . . ." said mam sighing. "I wish she was more of a cook like our Sandra. I'll bet she used every scrap of bread, too."

Then mam put her hand in her big brown handbag and took out a fifty pence piece. She gave the money to Jonny: "Before you dash off to that park, my laddo, you can just hop along to Marmood's and get a large white sliced loaf – and bring it straight back home." Then she hurried on, muttering something about getting someone to scrape all that toffee off the metal door handle – and what a disgrace it was. . . .

Jonny was fuming about the bread. "Why should *I* have to go for it?" he said to himself. "All those others guzzling bread the whole time – slice after slice, dad's bait box to take to the steel works – twelve slices. Bread for Albert's chip butties – a thousand slices. Bread pinched by Sandra for all those fat, over-fed pigeons at the bus

13

station – a million slices. Everyone using it up the whole time, and me – the youngest – having to spend hours and hours hauling it back from the shops! And anyway – mam should have got it. She should have got that bread. Mothers are supposed to do that."

His brow darkened as he thought of Marmood's shop and of all the time he'd have to waste waiting in a queue there. And by then it would be dark and the whole evening in the park would have been wasted!

As he thought all these things, he continued running. But not towards the shop – not at all! He was still running towards the park, and the Brown Brothers and Pam's brother Stew, and all the others who would be waiting for him.

When mam got in, she immediately went into the front room and looked through the lace curtains to check up on him.

"What on earth's he up to?" she said to Rita who was now putting her full weight onto the tortured arm of the best chair in the house as she sat varnishing her finger nails.

"I don't think Jonny's taken the slightest notice of me and that sliced loaf," said

mam. "He's going the wrong way . . . and
running too! I told him to go to the corner
shop and bring me back some bread before
it closes. I might as well talk to myself in
this house." Then she said in a very pained
voice: "And Rita, I do wish you wouldn't
sit on the arm of that chair. It's the only
decent one we've got."

Rita didn't move, but she raised her
eyebrows so that they looked like huge
railway arches and spread out her long
fingers like a fan. "No wonder the Briggs
family's got such a bad name at that school
of his," she said. "He never does a thing
he's told at home or school. I'd leave, if *I*
had to teach him. And I wouldn't let him
wear that stupid gold belt all the time
either. When I was at that school Mr
Badger never let *us* wear things like that!"

"Look, Rita," said mam in a dangerously
quiet voice, "I'm very tired, and your dad'll
be in soon. I thought you said *you* had to be
out by seven to see your friend Mavis. The
sooner you move, the better! I don't want
Mavis draping herself round this kitchen
while dad's trying to get a meal." Mam
stared at Rita's fingers: "This house is full
of your rubbish. Surely you aren't putting a

different colour on every nail?"

Rita scowled. Then she said aggressively, through her teeth with her mouth almost closed in a hard thin line, "Yes, mam. It's called the Blonde Harlequin look – specially for fair people like me. And I *was* supposed to be painting them gold, silver, lemon, orange and pearl – but all the lemon's gone thanks to *someone* using it to paint J.B. on a bedroom window. It's the most horrible thing in the world being a girl in this house! And just *you* mind you don't tip any of *my* stuff out, our mam!"

"You cheeky young hussy!" gasped mam. "I'm beginning to think dad's right about you. You're getting too big for your boots, my girl. And, if I remember rightly, I asked *you* to go for that bread before I went out this morning and you said you couldn't because you'd be late for school . . ."

Fifteen-year-old Rita and her mother glared at each other like warrior chiefs. . . .

Jonny was completely forgotten.

Mam was mad with Rita and she showed it by stamping into the kitchen and clanging pans about as she got dad's tea ready.

And Rita was mad with mam, and she showed it by thumping her way upstairs like a hundred rampaging elephants and slamming the bedroom door so hard that it nearly fell off its hinges and made the downstairs kitchen ceiling shake.

Then mam dashed out of the kitchen in a frenzy, and tore upstairs and battered the picture of the skater on the girls' bedroom door with her wooden rolling-pin and yelled at Rita to stop knocking the house to bits as it was the only one they'd got, and that if Rita wasn't satisfied she could go and live in a tent on Clareville common and good riddance to her!

Then mam calmed down and went back to the kitchen to put the kettle on . . .

2

It was one of those warm, still evenings in the park when voices seemed to echo in the slowly fading summer light.

As Jonny got near the great stretches of short green grass and tall trees he could hear the voices of his friends before he could see them. The scent of roses from near the tennis courts filled the air. Life was bliss!

Gradually he caught sight of the Brown brothers kicking a ball about in the far distance. He quickened his speed and sped towards them.

Then, suddenly, he stopped. "What's up?" shouted the Browns as they let the black and white ball roll to a standstill. "Get a move on! We've been waiting for you." Then, seeing him hesitating, one of them called: "What's up? Have you lost summat?"

Everyone stopped playing. They all crowded round Jonny.

"It's some money our mam gave me for bread. I just felt the fifty pence piece. I'll have to go back and get a sliced loaf or she'll go mad. We haven't any bread left and if there's no bread in the house it's murder."

Everyone looked very glum.

"Our Stew's due here any minute to play goalie against Saggo's lot from Berrythorn Avenue," said Pamela Dean. "But he'll just go off home again if we haven't got a good team together! We're depending on you – Jonny." Her long, silky, dark hair was tied back with a red boot lace and she was wearing footy boots – the same as her friend Angela. They both looked great.

"I'll just have to run all the way there and back as quick as lightning," said Jonny, with a resigned look. "Run and run – without stopping . . ."

"And then you'll be too breathless to play properly," groaned Pam. "You won't have any energy left. We can't let Saggo beat us. He's rubbish!"

Then Jonny spotted someone sitting on the park seat reading a book. It was Peter.

At first he just looked at Peter as if he was part of the scenery. Peter was always somewhere about – always with them but somehow always separate because he never actually joined in anything. But he watched things very carefully and knew what was going on. At this very minute he was looking as neat as if he was setting off for school on a Monday morning, with his shoes glowing with polish and his chestnut hair as smooth as a chestnut itself.

Jonny's face lit up. Peter always helped people. That's why everybody liked him. Jonny went over to him.

"Do us a favour, Pete," he said, "nip across to Marmood's shop in Port Street and get a loaf for us; then do us another good turn and knock at our door – the one with the toffee on the door handle and J. B. scratched on the door step . . . and give them the loaf and the change. Then come back here, and after the footy I'll treat you to chips and mushy peas from the ten pence Humph gave me."

Peter looked up, and at first he didn't seem to be taking any notice. That's

strange, thought Jonny, who'd expected him
to smile and dash off immediately!

Then Peter said: "I'd just got to the very
best bit of this ghost story. It's not the same
when you're interrupted!"

Jonny tried to curb his impatience. If
Peter didn't go it would ruin everything.
"Look Pete, if you dash off right now, the
ghost story will still be in your head when
you get back. If it isn't – well – you'll be
able to read that bit all over again which'll
make it even better if it's nice and scary!
Come on Pete, chips *and* mushy peas
remember."

"Not for ten pence," said Peter, suddenly getting up and grinning. "It'll work out at about one chip each. Mind my book for me then, while I'm away." And he took the fifty pence piece from Jonny and began to walk towards the park gates.

Jonny picked up the book. It was still open at a page with a picture on it. The picture showed a tall, deathly-white ghost with long chains on its wrists. It was standing between an arched wooden door and a gravestone. Jonny kept staring at the picture. He felt himself soaking it up like a sponge. He felt his short fair hair bristling on his cold tingly scalp. He couldn't take his gaze away from that page. He felt shivery in the warm evening air, and was vaguely aware of the rest of them calling him to hurry up, but he couldn't move.

He looked at the picture again. It was a very strange picture. Very old and creepy. Then he noticed something . . . something he recognised . . . it was the shape of the arched wooden door which came to a point at the top. *That* wasn't strange at all! It was just like the one in the high brick wall of the cemetery park near the football ground.

The cemetery park was an open garden

of grass and flowers and seats to sit on. But there were still some old gravestones propped against the walls, and near to them – almost unseen because of a huge sycamore tree that shaded it – was a small door with a pointed arch. . . .

"Come on!" shouted Pam. "Here's Stew. Don't just stand there gawping, Jonny!"

Quickly Jonny closed the book. Then he took off his golden belt and put it next to the book and went to join the game.

He was playing full-back, so he was close to Stew who was in goal.

There wasn't much to do at their end.

"We're too good for them – that's what," said Stew. "Six goals for us and all the action at that other end. We could almost pack up!"

Jonny nodded silently. He had hardly ever spoken to Stew in the whole of his life. You never talked much to people like Stew who might one day play for The Boro' . . . you just played your heart out when they were in your game.

But once Jonny's gaze drifted away from the activity at the other end as he caught sight of Peter coming back. Peter was hurrying towards them looking quite worried.

"Just look at him!" gasped Jonny unbelievingly.

Stew looked puzzled and shook his head and glanced away again, but Jonny was staring at Peter in fascinated horror.

His hair was no longer bird's-egg smooth. It looked as if it had been grabbed and tugged at. His shiny shoes were plastered with mud. His neat blue jersey was plastered with mud, too. Surely Peter hadn't been in trouble? He never got mixed up in anything. And most of all . . . surely he hadn't got into trouble because of doing him – Jonny – a good turn?

A sense of foreboding made him go all pale inside and weak at the knees. Just when it had been such a good trouble-free day as well. . . . Jonny closed his eyes and waited.

"Wake up Briggsy," said a voice next to him. It was Stew. The ball was actually coming up to their end.

The game was a walkover for Jonny's lot. Saggo's gang from Berrythorn Avenue were beaten seven-nil. But they swore they'd get their own back and that it was only because their proper Goalie had had to go to the dentist's. And they all ran off shouting: "We was robbed!" and, "It wasn't a fair game."

Then, after all the noise had died down, everyone started to look at Peter. "You look as if *you've* been playing footy, Pete!" said Pam.

Peter was spitting on his handkerchief and trying to wipe mud off himself with it. "Mam'll faint," he said anxiously. "She once nearly fainted when a tin of emulsion paint fell on me."

Jonny looked at him hard. He had never seen those neat clothes looking such a mess in all his life. But the main point was – had Pete got that loaf and taken it to Port Street? "Did you get the bread, Pete?"

Peter stopped wiping the mud off. "Yes, I got it. Here's the change." Then he said, "But I didn't take it back to your house, Jonny. This ghost thing grabbed it off me. It pushed me over in the back entry – next to Marmood's – and then it vanished with the bread . . ."

Ghost? Everyone was in an uproar. A *real* ghost? What did it look like?

Peter looked puzzled: "At first I thought it was a man with a sheet over his head and old black track shoes on his feet. Then it went away very quickly. It sort of melted into nowhere . . . I think it must have been

the ghost everyone's talking about. . . . A
real one . . . a *real* ghost . . ." Then he said:
"And don't forget those chips and mushy
peas, Jonny Briggs. It wasn't my fault the
ghost took the bread!"

Jonny groaned to himself. He was in the
dog-house now, and no mistake – no bread!
And, what's more, the bread money spent
as well. He began to think about joining the
army again, and never going home to Port
Street any more.

Nobody would care if I never went back,
he thought to himself. It would mean more
room in the bedroom for Humph and
Albert, and *much* more food for Albert and
a spare bit in the kitchen drawer to put his

tins of fishing maggots in. And even Sandra, the best one of the girls, wouldn't really care. And as for Rita . . . *she* would be over the moon with delight! She told him to *get lost* every day of his life!

Perhaps if he went to the Recruiting Officer at that shop in the town where the Army place was, he could ask them to take him on as a sort of army mascot – and make a mistake with his age – like eighteen instead of eight. . . . After all, some people of eighteen were as small as him . . . not many, but there were *some*.

He walked over to the seat where his gold belt was and put it on again. Peter followed him and picked up his book. Then, with the others, they wandered off towards the chip-shop.

The chip shop was just past the cemetery garden. As they walked past and saw the gravestones propped up round the brick walls at the side, Jonny told Peter about the door with the pointed arch.

"I saw it in that book of yours," he said. "And there's one exactly the same behind that sycamore tree in the brick wall over there!" He pointed excitedly to the other side of the cemetery park. "It's just like the one in the picture with the ghost and the gravestones!"

Then Peter said: "P'raps it's where the ghost that knocked me down lives . . ."

And everyone started chattering and talking very quickly about all the ghosts they'd seen and heard about.

The Brown brothers' Aunty May had seen the ghost of her dead sister. Nadine had seen the ghost of Miss Broom dressed in a long green nightie behind the school bicycle shed . . . and it wasn't a joke because she asked Miss Broom if she had a long green nightie and Miss Broom said yes.

Lily Spencer, whose mother was a nurse, said her mother knew more true ghost stories than anyone else alive. And Jonny himself said that Rita's friend Mavis was in love with a ghost who sang to her at night because her parents had stopped her having her stereo on after midnight.

"Perhaps it's true that the ghost that knocked Pete down lives in there," said Pam, pointing to the door. "Don't forget that lots of people say it's the ghost of a footballer with no head and a football under his arm. . . . And this garden's right near Ayresome Park football ground!"

There was a sudden silence and all of them stopped for a moment and stared towards the sycamore tree. Pamela shivered a bit, and even Jonny felt a bit uneasy. Then they all hurried on to the chip shop.

On the way out again when everyone was going home in different directions, Jonny Briggs said slowly: "Anyone want to come with me and walk past that door in the wall of the cemetery gardens?"

He had been thinking about the whole thing when he was eating his mushy peas. Thinking that he ought to try and find that ghost, clutching at his gold belt and saying to himself: If I don't find out about the ghost that knocked down Peter and pinched the bread, I might as well never go home again. Because if I can't find anything out, they'll never believe me at home. They'll never believe *me* if I go in and say: "Oh yes, mam . . I got the loaf, but this ghost pinched it down the back entry." They'd just laugh and call me a little liar – especially our Rita. But of course it's all right for them all to *say* there's a ghost and gabble their heads off about it. He even remembered mam mentioning it yesterday: "Yes," she'd said, "Mrs Prince across the road swears she saw it last night. It was all black with a blue light shining from it, and it was in the entry behind our house. She was off to the doctor's first thing, to get a bottle to calm her nerves. She said it was terrible!''

It was funny — thought Jonny — how everybody saw a different sort of ghost! But if *he* went and said he'd seen one — they'd all laugh and say he'd been imagining it. And the funny thing was that up to now, he did seem to be the only person that could truthfully say he'd never seen a ghost within a million miles!

But they still made his hair stand on end, those ghosts, and he still felt a bit frightened about going to hunt for one.

When Jonny mentioned walking past the door in the cemetery gardens, it had a curious effect. The Brown brothers ran off saying they'd just caught sight of their bus, three other people said their mothers would be wondering where they were, and all the girls except Pam said they weren't allowed to wander about streets at night and vanished in a flash. And within two minutes there was just Peter, hurrying away, still holding his book and stopping every now and again to brush his knees, and Pamela Dean, still standing next to him.

"I'll come with you," she said. "I'd like to tell our Stew I've seen the ghost of the headless footballer. He'll be green with envy. And then after that I'll have to run all the way home before it gets dark, so come on."

They both turned and hurried across a wide cobbled street towards the cemetery gardens again. There weren't many people about. The seats in the garden were empty, and dusk was beginning to creep across the sky. There was a warm, darkening stillness as they hurried along a smooth grey footpath, past the huge heavy gravestones – all sooty and moss-covered, with the writing on them nearly worn away. . . .

In front of them loomed a huge sycamore tree, and hidden beneath its deep green leaves was the door in the brick wall. . . . It was a wooden door, pointed at the top to fit into a stone archway. Dark maroon paint was curling off it and it had a huge black, ring-shaped handle.

Jonny and Pam stood in front of it for a few moments and stared. Then Jonny walked slowly towards the handle and tried to twist it to open the door. It would hardly move.

"Let me have a go," said Pam. She used all her strength to try to move the handle with both hands. It squeaked rustily.

Then Jonny had another go and this time there was a definite "click". They both pushed, and slowly the door moved. . . . They pushed again and this time it actually opened! It opened a couple of feet, and as they looked down to the ground Jonny could see grass and weeds, bits of coal and pieces of rotten wood. They opened it a bit more and stared in cautiously.

"It's a shed!" said Pam. "A shed full of rotten old rubbish. It looks as if it's been a coal-shed."

They both edged inside and looked round. The only window in it was a small roof light. In one corner there was an old table with a rusty tool box on it full of rusty nails, and in another corner was half a sack of coke. There was also an ancient lawn-mower and a brush with no bristles left.

"I can't imagine even a ghost wanting to be in here!" said Jonny, and he got hold of the lawn-mower and tried to move it, but it was thick with rust.

Pam picked up the sweeping brush and knocked down a cobweb with it. A rotten piece of shelf fell down with a clatter. She gave a gasp and shivered. "Come on then, let's get out. At least we know there's no ghost. . . ."

"Sh . . . sh . . ." said Jonny suddenly, "I can hear footsteps! It might be the police. We'll be in for it if they find us snooping round here. . . ." He dodged to the door and closed it carefully and as quietly as he could. Then he grinned. "Even the ghost won't be able to get in now," he said. The footsteps were quite loud now, getting nearer and nearer. Jonny and Pam stood in the semi-darkness, not daring to move.

The footsteps stopped right outside.

With one hand Jonny clutched his gold belt and with the other he held Pam's hand. He was holding his breath back so much that when he did breathe it came out all trembly. There was a slight cough just outside the door, then the footsteps moved on and faded away.

"Phew!" gasped Jonny at last. "That was a narrow escape! Just imagine if he'd opened the door and . . ." his voice began to falter. Without another word he walked

towards the door and peered at it. Pam was
looking at the door too.

"There's no handle on it . . ." she said.
"The handle has come off the door on the
inside. We can't open it!"

At first Jonny was absolutely dazed. He
stared at the place where that handle should
have been. All there was was a small, round
hole. He bent down to look into the hole,
and deep inside he could just see the spindle
which opened and closed the door. It was in
a small, dark tunnel, impossible to reach.

"Try poking a stick into it," said Pam.
"Then, perhaps, if we waggled the
stick. . . ."

But there was no stick. There was nothing
to fit it. Jonny couldn't quite take it in. He
had never been trapped in a place before.
He had often hidden in secret places – like
the airing cupboard at home, or in a corner
of the school yard. But he always chose
places he was sure of being able to get out
of, or away from. And now, for the first
time, he was a real prisoner.

Then Pam said: "It looks as if we're
trapped. We'd better start to shout and
bang on the door. It's funny that . . . a
minute ago we were hiding in case it was

the police and now I'd be quite glad if a policeman came and got us out!"

They both started to shout at the tops of their voices and batter at the door with the brush handle and scraps of wood. Gradually their voices got quieter and the knocking got slower. Nothing was happening, and it was getting so dark they could hardly see each other.

"We could try standing on the table and breaking the roof glass with the brush handle," said Jonny.

But Pam said no straight away to that: "We can't see what we're doing, properly," she said, "and broken glass flies everywhere. We might break that window and then be rescued all sliced up with bits of glass sticking in us." She gave a big sigh. "We'll just have to take it in turns at bashing the door and shouting. Thank goodness I had a double helping of chips, otherwise I'd be starving by now!"

Jonny nodded in the darkness. He was glad Pam was with him. It was better being a prisoner when there was a friend there. He began to wonder what they'd be doing at home. It must be nearly bed-time by now. . . . Dad and mam would have switched off the telly, and mam would have set the table ready for breakfast tomorrow. And dad would have thrown a couple of tea-bags at next door's cat if it was lurking at the back when he put the key under the plant-pot for anyone coming in late.

But he'd never be expecting Jonny – the youngest – to be coming in the latest! Just imagine them all going to bed before him, all lying there soft and comfortable while he and Pam stood in a little dark shed and waited for someone to rescue them. . . .

"It's a good job it isn't cold," Pam said. "Just supposing it was cold . . ." and she gave the door an extra loud bang, and kicked it, and yelled *help!* at the top of her voice.

Then they both yelled *help!* together.

3

At ten o'clock that same night, Jonny
Briggs's mam and dad began to get
worried. . . .

"He's not usually as late as this unless he
goes to the pictures with someone," said
mam to dad, "and he wasn't going to the
pictures when I saw him earlier on. And he
never brought that loaf in either." She put
her hands to her face and pressed her cheeks
very hard, and frowned. "I'm beginning to
wonder what's happened. . . ."

Dad had been fiddling with his cabbage
patch in the back yard nearly all evening,
but now he had come in and put the
television on, while mam made a pot of tea.

"It's these summer nights," said dad.
"He'll be busy playing in the park and have

forgotten the proper time . . ."

"And forgotten our bread, too!" said
mam. She was getting very nattery, now . . .
edgy, and nattery and bad-tempered. She
always got nattery when she was worried:
"I told him about that loaf distinctly! I
said, 'call at Marmood's and bring it
straight back here', and I gave him fifty
pence. . . . If he's gone off and spent that
money on something else, he'll feel the
weight of my hand on his backside the
minute he walks through that door!"

"Yes, yes. . . All right, love . ." said
dad, beginning to get a bit narky himself.
"I think you've said all that about four
times already tonight, lass, so how about a
bite to eat eh? How about a nice, fat,
corned beef sandwich with scallions and a
dash of salad cream?"

"But I keep telling you . . ." said mam,
almost at her wit's end, "THERE ISN'T ANY
BREAD LEFT! And I've no intention of
borrowing any either. Why do you think
I've been going on like this? You'll just
have to have cold rice pudding if you're
really hungry – and tomorrow for breakfast
it'll be cornflakes and six cream crackers to
share between the lot of us!"

Dad drank his tea in silence. Then he looked at the clock. "Mmm," he said, "it does seem to be getting a bit late."

Just then, Albert came in, followed by Humph.

"Seen anything of our Jonny?" asked dad.

"Not a thing, fortunately," said Albert going straight to the bread bin.

"It's no use looking in there tonight, Albert," said mam dryly.

Albert groaned and pushed back his floppy hair with his bony hand. "How is it there's never any food in this house?" he said. Then he took a giant bag of crisps out of his pocket and began eating them.

"I saw our Jonny playing footy in the park," said Humph, "but it was about two hours ago and the park's empty now."

"Do you think someone ought to go and try to find him?" said mam.

"Try and *find* him?" exploded Albert spraying crisps everywhere. "What on earth for?"

"I'll go if you like," said Humph, and he set off out again.

At the corner of Port Street, Humph met Rita and her friend Mavis. They were both

wearing gigantic wire earrings and Rita was
saying to Mavis: "I liked that one in the
velvet jacket with the deep croaky voice. He
plays the guitar too. . . . He said he thinks
I'd fit in with their sort of group very well."

"Seen anything of our Jonny?" said
Humph.

Rita stopped dead in her tracks and
stared at him as if he had just landed from
outer space: "Our Jonny . . .?"

"Yes, you know," said Humph sarcastically, "that kid brother of yours. The square one with the short bristly fair hair. The one you love so much . . ."

Rita shrugged her shoulders silently, but Mavis suddenly said: "I didn't see him – but I saw that friend of his – the one that always wears that neat blue pullover. He was all covered in mud and said he'd been attacked by a ghost in the alley behind Marmood's shop and this ghost had stolen a loaf of bread."

"And what's that got to do with us?" said Rita.

"It was just that he said he was going back to your Jonny in the park," said Mavis.

Humph frowned slightly and his monkey face became a mass of lines: "Did you say, 'a ghost' Mavis?"

"That's what I *thought* he said . . ." said Mavis nervously, and she began to go all pink.

"Did he say what the ghost was like?"

"No," said Mavis, "he just went on and on about how the ghost had taken his loaf."

"Come *on*, Mave," said Rita, "we can't stay talking to him all night. Come on back to our house and I'll make us both one of those French Salad sandwiches with lots of onion in. We don't need to worry the same about eating onions when there's just the two of us!"

"You won't find much bread to eat with them," shouted Humph as he hurried away.

Jonny and Pam were beginning to get very tired in the shed. It was dark and very quiet. Occasionally they heard the sound of cars in the distance and a dog barking, but apart from that there was nothing: even when they banged as hard as they could and shouted at the tops of their voices.

Jonny began to shiver a bit. "Supposing they *never* come to rescue us?" he said.

But Pam was more cheerful. "My mam and dad wouldn't let me stay lost," she said. "They'd go to the police and put notices in the paper and on television. Somebody's sure to let us out in the end – even if we have to wait till the morning when there are people in the park again."

Then Jonny had a new idea. "Why don't we try pulling the lawn-mower to the door and tipping it up a bit so that it moves along on its two wheels. Then we could bash it really hard against the door so that it makes a hole in it."

In the darkness they puffed and panted as they tried to move the rusty lawn-mower, and at last they got it near to the door. Jonny pressed down on the two metal handles so that it tipped up slightly and rolled on its two big wheels, then he pushed it with all his might against the door of the hut. But it was no use! The door of the hut was very thick and sturdy and the metal lock had been built to last.

He turned away from the door, almost sick with disappointment and fear. It was all very well for Pam to say they'd be rescued in the end, but just think of all the fuss and the trouble there'd be if the police had to be called in and it was in the papers or on television! Everyone would be on to them. Mr Badger at school would give everybody a lecture about trespassing on private property and as usual, he, Jonny Briggs would be in trouble again, in boiling hot trouble! It might even effect his chances of playing football again with Stew. Stew, and Pam's mam and dad, weren't going to be very pleased that Pam had gone ghost hunting with him. And everyone would say

that there weren't such things as ghosts –
even though lots of *them* secretly believed in
them. . . .

As he thought all this, he suddenly
noticed something blood-curdlingly
horrible. . . . There was something else in
the shed with them. . . .

Something was slowly starting to move in
the corner of the shed . . . there was a
shuffling sound as if a dark, unknown
creature was unwinding itself from the
depths of the blackness. It was the corner of
the shed they hadn't been able to see
properly before, because the lawn-mower
had been there.

Almost trembling, Jonny clutched Pam's
arm. His voice was hoarse and cracked and
only one word came out: "Mmonster . . ."

They were both frozen like icicles. Frozen
on a warm summer's night. Paralysed with
fear as The Thing moved about in the
corner.

"A rat monster," gulped Pam. "One of
those giant rats that escaped from that
travelling circus last week. . . ."

They both stood – not daring to move,
peering into the blackness to try and make
out whether their worst fears were correct.

It was Jonny who acted first this time. He picked up a piece of rotten wood to defend himself. And not a second too soon because the shape was moving slowly out of the corner towards them.

Jonny hurled the piece of wood at the shape with all his might. There was a loud and terrible squalking and the shape spun into the air! It leapt onto the old wooden table, knocking nails and old boxes and bits of wood in all directions. A pair of big yellow eyes loomed up at them angrily.

"It's a moggy!" said Pam. "A big, black, gigantic moggy! How on earth did it get in here?"

They both stared towards the corner where the cat had been. The corner looked quite light, quite strange. . . .

"There's a hole there!" gasped Jonny. "A hole in the rotten wood."

"It's not thick wood like the door in the wall," said Pam. "It's old, thin, rotten wood!"

Then they both struggled with the rusty lawn-mower, moved it round from the door and tried to push it against this small hole in the rotting wall of the shed. And at last, things started to happen! There was the

sound of splintering wood and the old lawn-
mower ploughed straight through the
wooden wall – splintering and cracking all
the wood as it went.

Then they dragged it back again.

They were both panting by now and
feeling hot with all the struggling and the
thought of getting out at last. They pulled
the lawn-mower out of the way. It had left
a hole just big enough for them to wriggle
through!

"You go first," said Jonny to Pam.
"You're a bit smaller. But watch out for
splinters . . ." They squiggled and wriggled
and pushed themselves through the hole,
scratching their legs on bits of wood and
dragging soft black earth and dead twigs
and rotting leaf-mould against their
stomachs. But they shuffled forward until
they were clear of that awful wooden shed.

Then they both stood upright and
breathed deeply in the darkness of the
summer night, breathed with relief and
smelled cool damp scent of the earth and
the lingering presence of the flowers in the
cemetery gardens.

Suddenly they were aware of a
completely different world. The world of
sleeping people, with only them awake. . . .

"We'll both have to walk home, now,"
said Jonny. "Shall I come back with you
first, in case you can't get in? I'll hide
behind the hedge at the corner of your road
and wait to see if you get in all right . . ."

Pam nodded and they set off.

There were orange street lights along the
main road to her house. But there was no
traffic on the roads. It was all very quiet
and ghostly and all there was to be seen was

one stray dog wandering about.

They had nearly got to Pam's house in Parkland Road when they heard running footsteps. They both dodged behind a tree in a front garden. The person running began to get nearer. He was wearing a track suit.

"It's our Stew!" gasped Pam. "He must have been running all over town looking for me. I'll creep out of this garden and pretend I haven't seen him. You wait here until we've both gone in, then make a run for it."

Pam dodged out of the garden and began to walk to her house. Jonny saw Stew catch her up and faintly he heard Stew asking her where on earth she'd been and he heard her say that a whole lot of them had got trapped in this old wooden shed when they'd been ghost hunting.

Thank goodness she didn't just say there was only me, breathed Jonny. Thank goodness she didn't mention any names!

Soon he saw lights going on all over the place in Pam's house, and the front door opened and he heard a man's voice swearing. Then Stew and Pam disappeared and the door closed behind them.

4

Quietly, Jonny left the garden and slid
like a small shadow along the garden hedges
until he was at the main road with the
orange lights again. Then he dashed along
it as if a hundred demons were after him
and eventually got to Port Street without
being seen by anyone.

He gave a huge sigh of heartfelt relief. So
far – so good. But what was it going to be
like when he actually tried to get into his
own house at this late hour?

He began to wonder whether to go to the
front door and knock in an ordinary casual
way, or whether to sneak round the back
and throw pebbles at a window. It would
be just his luck to throw something and it
would break the window, then there would

be even *more* trouble!

He stood for a second and looked at his front door. The toffee looked all dark on the door handle and the empty milk bottles glinted a bit in the blackness by the side of the doorstep. The windows had a strange blank look because all the curtains were drawn, and they looked lighter in the dark of the night . . . all white and ghostly. . . . Suddenly Jonny felt small and strange and alone. Then he heard next door's tom-cat starting to have a fight and things seemed all right again, and he grinned as he thought of the other cat in the shed and how they'd thought it was a monster . . . I expect in some ways they *are* monsters, he thought to himself, I expect it depends if you're a mouse or not . . . and in a way me and Pam were a bit like mice trapped in that shed.

Then he went round to the back entry. I'll try going in the back way, he thought.

The houses in Jonny's street all had back entries and high brick walls to the backyards with oblong wooden doors. Most people locked their wooden doors from the inside, last thing at night, so it was pretty well impossible to get through.

Jonny crept cautiously towards his own backyard door. He knew it in the darkness because there was a small panel of wood missing from near the bottom of the door. A panel just big enough to let in all the stray animals of the area but not big enough for a boy to wriggle through.

The door *seemed* to be fastened when he got up to it.

He could just see the back bedroom windows too. The curtains were drawn and the house was as silent as the grave. . . .

He stood for a moment. He thought, I'll check the yard door just to make sure it's really locked and barred . . . then I might try climbing over. But he knew it wasn't very easy climbing over because the wall was high and the door was smooth on the outside. . . . Perhaps he ought to go back to the front after all.

He was just thinking this when he heard a noise. It wasn't a tom-cat or a dog this time. It sounded like someone moving about quietly. For a moment he felt quite glad. Perhaps it was Humph – on the look-out for him. He could always rely on Humph to come to his rescue . . .

But then . . . somehow that didn't make

sense. If Humph didn't even know he was
there – why would he be moving about so
quietly in their backyard? Jonny felt
extremely puzzled and a bit afraid.

He bent down, and peered through the
small gap in the yard door to try and
fathom out just exactly what was going on.
And when he saw – his heart nearly missed
a beat! For a ghost was standing in the
backyard . . . a white headless ghost . . .!

Jonny almost slipped to the ground in unbelieving amazement.

Then he put his face to the gap in the wood again and looked. Yes! It was definitely a ghost. A headless white ghost! And it was holding something under its arm . . . something round.

Jonny could feel the blood racing round his body. He could feel his cheeks tingling with excitement. He didn't feel a bit frightened now. He just felt triumphant that at last he had seen the ghost that everybody had been talking about for so long, and in his very own backyard too.

He gripped his gold belt. He felt ready for anything! What sort of a ghost would it be? Would it be a friendly one or a miserable one? A lot of ghosts were very sad, miserable creatures who had had unhappy lives. Would it be able to talk and tell him its life story, or would it just moan and rattle its chains?

He bent down and took another look through the crack. One thing was certain – this one didn't have any chains to rattle. And as it was headless, it probably wouldn't be able to talk to him or even groan . . . that was probably why it was moving about so quietly with its head tucked underneath its arm.

Head under its arm? No, that wasn't right, surely? That was just what their Rita had said. The real people who *knew* said it was the ghost of a headless footballer with a *football* under his arm. Then he began to wonder if headless footballers could sign autographs and if it was worth trying to get in the house for a bit of paper and a pencil – then out again into the yard to see if the ghost would give Jonny Briggs his autograph. And if that happened – Jonny Briggs would be in the *Guinness Book of Records* for having the autograph of the ghost of a headless footballer (although when the Boro' lost – dad sometimes said the whole team was headless)!

With the idea of the autograph still in his mind, Jonny crept away from the back entry and went round to the front of his house in Port Street. But he didn't knock. He called through the letter box. . . . a hoarse, harsh cry: "Huu . . . . umph . . ." He tried to make it as muffled as he could so that if mam and dad were asleep they'd think he was already in and just calling for Humph in his sleep.

And – miracle of miracles – it actually worked!

Humph was at that door in a flash – almost as if he had been listening all the time at the top of the stairs. "Where in Hell's name have you been?" he said. He almost sounded like mam! "The whole place has been searching for you. They've all given you up except mam, dad and me! The girls and Albert are snoring their heads off. But not dad and mam – oh no! They're in a real panic! Thinking you've been knocked down by a car and all sorts. Been round to Middlesbrough General. Been to the police station twice, and this time *they're* not back yet. It's three o'clock in the morning don't forget!"

Jonny pushed his way in excitedly: "P'raps it's just as well mam and dad aren't here," he whispered: "Because there's a ghost in our backyard and I want to get its autograph. Quick – where's a pencil and some paper?"

"Hold on," said Humph, beginning to scowl a bit, "have you gone mad or something? Anyway, what have you been up to all this time since I saw you in the park just after tea?"

But Jonny just hadn't time to explain. His thoughts were on that ghost. "Paper," he said, "and a pencil! It's true – it's the ghost of a footballer – a headless one with a football underneath his arm and he's in *our backyard this minute!* Go and look through the window if you don't believe me – only be careful. We don't want to disturb him. . . ."

Jonny and Humph went into the kitchen, and peered carefully between the crack in the curtains.

Humph could hardly believe his eyes: "You're right!" he gasped. "Somebody with a white sheet over his head in our backyard. . . ."

"It's a GHOST," said Jonny, "with a football under its arm." Then he hesitated and looked closer: "A ghost with *two* footballs under its arm. . . ."

"Cabbages – you mean," said Humph calmly. "Two of our dad's biggest cabbages under his arm!" Then he said: "Of all the swindling devils – pinching cabbages from a backyard!"

Jonny Briggs's heart sank. Pinching cabbages. What a let-down! So he wasn't going to get the autograph of a headless footballer after all. What a terrible disappointment! Then he began to feel *really* angry! How dare someone dress up as a ghost and make everyone look a lot of fools! How dare someone get everyone thinking . . . and wondering . . . and imagining . . . and describing . . . and explaining and talking about ghosts, when really it was some mean, mangy, ordinary, sly pincher – creeping about dressed in a sheet at the dead of night! Then, he suddenly remembered the loaf and what Peter had said at first – that he thought it looked like a man with a sheet over his head. So this – this *creature* snooping about among the cabbages in their backyard was probably the same one that had knocked down Peter and pinched the bread!

"We must catch him . . ." said Humph, moving quietly away from the kitchen window. "The best plan would be for me to creep out to him in the yard – and for you to go out round to the entry again – and wait at our backyard door in case he tries to bolt through it. Then, if he does try to get through, at least you could try and grab the sheet off him and find out who he really is."

Jonny nodded reluctantly. But it wasn't the same any more. It wasn't the same if it was only a person with a sheet over their head. It wasn't as exciting as if it had been a real ghost.

Fancy trying to catch a human being with cabbages under his arm instead of the ghost of a footballer! It had spoilt everything. . . .

"Hurry up then!" said Humph, giving him a gentle push. "We don't want him to get away without even a scuffle!"

Quickly, Jonny nipped off round the back again and waited at the yard door. He stood quietly for a moment. . . . then he bent down and looked through the gap in the door again. Yes – it was still there . . . and – it *was* a proper ghost . . . he was ready to swear to it! A proper ghost with something under its arm. A headless ghost!

I wish I'd got that bit of paper and pencil after all, he thought to himself. It doesn't do to have other people telling you you're wrong and that it isn't a real ghost, even when it's our Humph telling you. It's best to believe your own eyes."

It seemed ages before he heard Humph open the back door and come out into the yard. At any other time he would almost have gone to sleep waiting. But this time it was just the opposite. Here he was, in the middle of the night and he felt completely wide awake. He felt more wide awake than he'd ever felt in his life before. His eyes felt as round and as staring as huge gob stoppers because he felt so wide awake . . . and he stood there like a wide-awake statue . . . ready to grab at the person who had pinched dad's cabbages, or at a real ghost with a football under its arm.

The next thing that happened was very strange indeed and Jonny will never forget it for the rest of his life. He heard Humph open their back door. It was all happening – just as Humph had said it would – except he had really expected to hear some sort of scuffling or somebody shouting or cursing because they'd been caught.

But there was nothing like that at all. Jonny was very puzzled. He stood and waited patiently, ready to hurl himself forward the moment anyone tried to get out of the yard door or climb over the wall . . . but all was complete silence. . . .

Then he had this strange sensation. He felt something coming towards him. He felt as if he was being drawn towards something . . . and something was being drawn towards him, like two magnets. Yet all the time he was just standing there by the back entry door.

How can anything be coming towards me, he thought, when I've got this brick wall in front of me and that door's shut?

Then he felt a cold shaft of air across his face, not ordinary summer air but cold, dark, musty air; air a bit like that in the hut where he and Pam had been trapped. Jonny blinked uneasily, and as he blinked, a tall ghostly shape loomed up in front of him . . . just loomed and hovered like a glowing white mass until in the end he, Jonny Briggs, was right in the middle of it! It was like being in a strange, brightly-lit white fog . . . but cold, freezingly cold! A shimmering white kind of coldness like the bottom of the deep freeze at the supermarket. And he seemed to be frozen too. He meant to grab at the whiteness quickly – to make a grab at the ghost. But his hands were all stiff and cold as they tried to clutch. Then, as he looked at his hands to see what they were clutching, he saw they were clutching nothing at all. . . . His fingers were slowly opening and closing

in the night-time darkness. And there wasn't a soul except himself about . . . and a faint cold mustiness gently blowing on a sudden night breeze.

Then he heard Humph's voice and Humph rushing to the backyard door and swinging it open. "Did you manage to grab at him then?" breathed Humph excitedly. "I'm willing to bet my bottom teeth it was Arnold Jax who's living rough on Newport wasteland! He's been there since he had that row at home about the stolen lead from the church roof and cleared off. I'd know those black track shoes with the paint spilt on them anywhere, even in this bad light. I can tell by the way he walks too, the big scrounger!"

Jonny just stared at Humph, he was speechless.

"Do you mean to say you didn't even *try* to stop him?" said Humph. "Don't just stand there. Have you been struck dumb or what? Your eyes are nearly popping out of their sockets!" Then Humph said: "Ah well, I expect you're too tired, that's what it is. You'd better have a drink and get to bed. I'll wait up and see mam and dad."

They went inside and Humph made

Jonny a cup of cocoa. "You look as if you
need that," he said. "Your teeth are
chattering!"

In between sips of cocoa, Jonny told
Humph about Peter and the loaf, and about
him and Pam being trapped in the shed.

"In other words, you've had a real
ghostly night . . ." said Humph grinning.

But Jonny wasn't grinning back. *He* knew
he'd seen a proper ghost, and that it wasn't
just Arnold Jax with a sheet over his head.

Admittedly, it looked as if Arnold Jax could
well have knocked Peter down and pinched
that loaf. And Arnold Jax was just the sort
to lift a couple of cabbages from a
backyard. But Arnold Jax couldn't glow
with *coldness* . . . never in a month of
Sundays. . . . Arnold Jax couldn't *flow*
through a backyard wall and hang about in
a white foggy mist and smell all old and
musty. . . . Never!

Jonny followed Humph into the kitchen
and sat on a stool, still shivering a bit, while
Humph made the cocoa. Then Humph
poured it out.

"I've given you the one with the most
milk and sugar in," he said calmly,
"because you need it. And then, you want
to get off to bed quick! Before mam and
dad arrive. Don't worry about them . . . I'll
soon smooth them out. . . ."

Jonny sighed with relief. Thank goodness
there was someone like Humph in the house
when times were bad. He was as good as his
mother when she was in a good temper and
feeling kind. He was as good as his mother
when his mother wasn't fussing round the
girls or listening to the poisonous tales of
their Rita. In fact, sometimes he thought

that Humph was even *better* than his
mother, because he was even prepared to
stand up for him against all the rest of
them. . . .

Thankfully he drained the mug of cocoa
to the very last drop, then ran his finger
round the bottom of the mug to get the last
bit of sugar. Then he went off to bed. He
was just climbing into bed, next to a loudly
snoring Albert, when he heard the front
door opening and the voices of mam and
dad.

Everyone was home at last . . .

He put both his fingers in his ears to blot
out everything and screwed his eyes tight
shut. And soon the gentle warmth of
Albert's body next to him lulled him into a
happy contented sleep.

5

But downstairs it was different! Downstairs in that kitchen there was pandemonium! Mam was nearly having hysterics. "Just look at that clock!" she said. "Nearly four o'clock in the morning and us having to be up again in two hours' time! Just because our Jonny chooses to make a little fool of himself doesn't mean that the world comes to an end. Your poor dad still has to get to work as usual. I've still got to get up and get the breakfasts and get myself out as well. I'll never forget this dance he's led your poor dad and me . . ." All the time mam was talking she was glaring at Humph.

Humph listened in silence. His monkey face was very solemn. He was a born diplomat. He knew just when to speak and when not to speak.

As for dad, he didn't say much, but he looked very tired. His big, heavy face looked pale. "The lad's back. That's the main thing," he said. "Are there any of those cans of Newcastle Brown left in the back of the cupboard? I could do with a tin of 'Newki' right this minute."

Mam went to the cupboard to look. But all the time she was going on and on about how the whole of Cleveland police force was just about to launch a massive search for their son and how it meant someone would have to trail out yet again and tell them that everything was all right. Then she launched on to her favourite theme of how girls weren't half as much trouble to bring up as boys and how never in her whole life had any of the girls been out of the house as late as this.

Humph looked at her placidly and said: "Except our Rita of course . . . when she went to Blackpool on the football bus with that boy friend she had. Except when she missed the bus back and hitched a lift from a milk tanker and got back here at half-past five in the morning."

Then Humph put the kettle on and made

them a cup of tea and dad nipped out to
tell the police everything was O.K. And by
half-past four they were all sorted out and
really ready for bed!

"So you see," said Humph as they went
upstairs, "it was really Arnold Jax who was
to blame. He was the one who knocked that
kid down who'd been for our bread . . . and
tried to pinch our cabbages. He only got
one cabbage though – he dropped the other
on the way out of the yard. . . ."

"If our Jonny had done as he was told in
the first place," said mam, "none of it
would have happened. He had no right to
go dashing off to that park when I'd told
him to come straight back with the
bread . . ."

"Look, love," said dad wearily, "all that's
over now. It's all past. It all happened
yesterday. What we've got to do now is to
suffer the cornflakes and six cream crackers
to share between the lot of us. And once
that's over we can get back to normal!"

And with that they both went into their
bedroom and shut the door.

The next morning, you should have seen all
those faces in the kitchen!

Dad was crunching manfully at cornflakes
as if he was eating sand from Redcar beach.
Mam was fluttering round looking for a
packet of aspirins because she had a bad
head. Pat was dropping cream cracker
crumbs on a new salmon pink skirt and
looking at a catalogue for ice-skates, while
Sandra was trying to make her cream
cracker more interesting by garnishing it
with curry powder and sliced cucumber.
Albert was complaining about a funny
dream he'd had and how everything smelt
damp and musty in their bedroom because

of wet mud and old rotting leaves on Jonny's shoes under the bed, and Rita was happily drinking lemon juice and nibbling a slimming biscuit because she never ate a proper breakfast in any case.

"I never heard a thing . . ." said Rita. "Fancy him causing mam and dad all that trouble! There's nothing but trouble where he is. Poor old dad, so tired and having to work so hard in that steel works." Then she added innocently: "Oh – by the way, dad, do you think you could lend me three pounds to get this special Educational Record for school? We're going to play all these educational records tracing the growth of the modern music industry . . ."

"That's a new one, Rita," said Humph. "Educational records. Very educational if you ask me."

"Nobody *did* ask you – did they?" said Rita glaring at him. Then she turned and belted dad with a smile like a ray gun.

"Sorry love," he said, "I've no change at the moment." (He always said that when he didn't want to part with his money.) And with that, Rita flounced out of the kitchen saying that the whole of the Briggs family were a lot of Philistines who knew nothing about culture or education – and had anybody seen her eye-shadow?

"What's a Philistine?" said Albert, rubbing some mud off his shoe with his elbow.

"It's a rude, ignorant, mean person who isn't interested in artistic things!" yelled Rita. "And I've just found my eye-shadow, all trodden on, on the landing. If someone's been at it – I'll murder them!" And about two minutes later she thumped down the stairs and dashed off down the street to the Sixth-Form College.

Then dad suddenly said: "Where's our Jonny? Where's the cause of all last night's hullabaloo?"

Jonny, in the bedroom, heard this. He had very sharp ears. Somehow he didn't feel like going down and facing them all. He put on his faded old jeans and his grey jersey. Then he caught sight of his gold belt lying on the chair and it seemed to cheer him up. It was the best thing he'd ever made, and he'd done it all himself. But he didn't put it on for school today though, he tucked it away under a pile of comics instead. It was too precious to get lost.

The sun was hinting that it might rise

very high in the sky later on. He looked out
of the window on to the backyard and the
cabbage patch. It seemed as if it was going
to be a nice day. So, he took off his old grey
jumper and put on a T-shirt of Albert's that
had shrunk and just fitted him. It was a
nice blue colour and he liked it.

Then he looked out of the window again
and suddenly he stood as still as if he were
about to have his photograph taken. There
was something lying there, down among the
cabbages . . . cabbages with black crumpled
leaves. Black trodden earth where cabbages

were missing, and cabbages that looked as if
a tornado had hit them. It was a leather
football. . . . He had never seen it before in
his life.

He rushed downstairs. "There's a football
in the backyard!" he yelled as he tore out of
the back door.

The rest of them looked as if they had
been struck by a whirlwind. "Whatever's
got into him *now*?" said mam.

But Humph realised what Jonny was
getting at, and he too hurried out into the
yard. Then, even dad followed. He never
could resist a football, of any sort.

"Well, well," laughed dad (and he only

said that when he was absolutely amazed),
"fancy seeing one of those after all these
years! That must be like the footballs they
had nearly a hundred years ago! Now who
could have thrown a thing like that into our
backyard?" He picked it up and examined
it more closely. "Smells a bit funny too – all
damp and musty." Then he grinned and
handed it to Jonny: "There won't be many
kids in Middlesbrough with a football as old
as that. You'll be able to start a football
museum of your own with that!"

Then dad went off to work. He never
even mentioned last night, or having to
hunt for Jonny, or anything.

Humph looked at the football too.
"Strange that . . ." he admitted. "Very,
very strange. I wonder if Arnold Jax
dropped it when I chased him last night?
Maybe he found it on a rubbish dump
somewhere?"

"Of course he didn't find it on a rubbish
dump," said Jonny. "The ghost left it –
didn't he? The ghost left it just to show that
he really *was* a ghost . . ."

"Maybe you're right," said Humph
slowly. "Perhaps the ghost was your ghost."
Then he said: "You see Jonny, I somehow

can't believe in ghosts, so I think it was
Arnold Jax who dropped it. But just because
I don't believe in them, doesn't mean
there are no such things as ghosts . . . It's all
very complicated." Then Humph grinned
and went off to school himself, and Jonny
took the football and put it under their bed.

But not before his mother had tried to
stop him. "Where on earth are you going
with that dirty old thing?" she said. "You
never know where it's been. And if it's as
old as you say it is it could be covered with
germs and goodness knows what . . ." But
she didn't have time to go on because she
thought she heard someone tinkering with
the milk bottles and ran to the front door to
have a look, so Jonny was able to get
upstairs with it.

How absolutely amazing, he thought to
himself as he hurried down Port Street on
his way to school. Just wait till I tell Pam
and the rest of them!

The first person he saw as he got into the
school yard was Pam.

"I nearly wasn't going to be here this
morning," she said. "Mam wanted me to
have the morning off because of being in so
late and being in that shed. She was going

to write a long letter to Mr Badger telling him all about it, but I put her off. Pity we didn't see the ghost though. . . ."

Jonny grinned, "I did," he said proudly.

"You did?" The pink satin ribbons which Pamela Dean was wearing that morning seemed to quiver with excitement. Her eyes became round and wondrous. "You don't mean you actually saw . . . *You* . . . How . . . when?"

Then Jonny told her everything that had happened. And there was so much to say that they both got told off for talking.

"Jonny Briggs," said Miss Broom, "what was I just saying then about the people who live in Tibet?" Jonny felt his cheeks going scarlet. He had no idea about the people who live in Tibet because he had just got up to telling Pam about the football the ghost had left behind. . . .

Miss Broom glared at Pamela: "Pamela –

perhaps *you* can stand up and tell me about the people who live in Tibet?"

Pamela went as red as a beetroot too and stared at the top of her desk.

"Sit down," said Miss Broom, "and for goodness sake – please pay more attention!"

"Yes, Miss Broom," said Pam.

Then Miss Broom said: "If you all get on and pay attention to what I'm telling you about Tibet, and if you will get your written work finished properly – there *may* be time for a story. And if Jonny Briggs behaves himself – I *may* let him choose the story. . . ."

Jonny fixed Miss Broom with his full, undivided attention from that moment on. . . .

And I know what sort of a story it's going to be, he said to himself . . . It's just *got* to be a ghost story. . . . Just got to be . . . and he smiled happily.

More Jonny Briggs titles available from BBC/Knight

Jonny Briggs

Jonny Briggs and the Whitby Weekend

Jonny Briggs and the Great Razzle Dazzle

Jonny Briggs and the Giant Cave

Jonny Briggs and the Galloping Wedding

Jonny Briggs and the Jubilee Concert

The World of Jonny Briggs